BIG JOBS, BIG TOOLS!

AWESOME AIRCRAFT CARRIERS

MARIE ROGERS

New York

Published in 2022 by The Rosen Publishing Group, Inc.
29 East 21st Street, New York, NY 10010

Portions of this work were originally authored by Kenny Allen and published as *Aircraft Carriers*. All new material in this edition was authored by Marie Rogers.

First Edition

Editor: Greg Roza
Cover Design: Michael Flynn
Interior Layout: Rachel Rising

Photo Credits: Cover, pp.1, 5 Stocktrek Images/Stocktrek Images/Getty Images; pp. 4, 6, 8, 10, 12, 14, 16, 18, 20, 21 (background) 13Imagery/Shutterstock.com; p. 7 U.S. Navy/Handout/Getty Images News/Getty Images; p. 9 U.S. Navy/Handout/Hulton Archive/Getty Images; p. 11 Tom Stoddart Archive Contributor/Hulton Archive/Getty Images; p. 13 Jason and Bonnie Grower/Shutterstock.com; p. 15 Zack Frank/Shutterstock.com; p. 17 Chris Ison - PA Images/Contributor/PA Images/Getty Images; p. 19 FANTHOMME Hubert/Contributor/Paris Match Archive/Getty Images; p. 21 Stocktrek Images/Getty Images.

Cataloging-in-Publication Data

Names: Rogers, Marie.
Title: Awesome aircraft carriers / Marie Rogers.
Description: New York : PowerKids Press, 2022. | Series: Big jobs, big tools! | Includes glossary and index.
Identifiers: ISBN 9781725326576 (pbk.) | ISBN 9781725326590 (library bound) | ISBN 9781725326583 (6 pack)
Subjects: LCSH: Aircraft carriers–Juvenile literature.
Classification: LCC V874.R64 2022 | DDC 359.9'4835–dc23

Manufactured in the United States of America

CPSIA Compliance Information: Batch #CSPK22. For Further Information contact Rosen Publishing, New York, New York at 1-800-237-9932.

CONTENTS

Giant Machines

Aircraft carriers are big ships! They can be as long as skyscrapers are tall. That's because they need to be big enough to carry an entire air force. An air force is part of the **military**.

70

Aircraft carriers are floating air bases. They carry jets and sailors to places around the world. The largest aircraft carriers hold up to 100 jets. These large ships can carry 6,000 people!

JFK

Steel Boat

Aircraft carriers are made of steel. Their top is very wide. The part under the water is much narrower. Inside are different levels called decks. There are over 4,000 rooms on many aircraft carriers.

The Flight Deck

The flight deck is on the top of an aircraft carrier. It's where jets take off and land. Sailors work on the flight deck. Some make sure the people who fly jets are safe.

VFA 113
304

Speed Machines

Catapults make sure jets get up to speed. The jets must go fast to create enough lift to take off. When landing, jets slow down with the help of **hooks** and strong cables.

In the Island

Officers work in the island. They make sure things run smoothly. Other sailors direct the ship. **Radar** on the island helps the crew find enemies. Officers use radio **antennas** to talk to people flying jets.

67
BEWARE OF JET BLAST
PROPELLERS AND ROTORS

The Hangar

The deck below the flight deck is called the hangar. It's big enough to store more than 60 jets. Jets can be moved between the hangar and the flight deck with giant elevators.

Powering a Ship

On the lowest deck, there are strong engines, or machines that create power, and a power plant. These move the boat with four giant **propellers**. They power the lights and machinery on the ship too.

A Floating City

Aircraft carriers are cities at sea. They have everything people need. Sailors live on the middle decks. Mess halls serve up to 18,000 meals a day. There's a post office, hospital, barbershop, and more!

USS *Gerald R. Ford*

Length: 1,092 feet (332.9 m)

Flight deck width: 256 feet (78 m)

Weight: nearly 100,000 tons (90,718.5 mt)

Home to more than 4,500 sailors at a time

Carries 75 aircraft at a time

GLOSSARY

antenna: A metal device used to send or receive radio or TV signals, or messages.

catapult: A device for launching an airplane from the deck of a ship.

hook: A curved device (such as a piece of bent metal) for catching, holding, or pulling something.

military: Armed forces, or relating to armed forces.

propeller: A device having a hub fitted with blades that is made to turn quickly by an engine and that causes a ship, powerboat, or airplane to move.

radar: A machine that uses radio waves to locate and identify objects.

FOR MORE INFORMATION

WEBSITES

Build Watercraft
pbskids.org/designsquad/blog/why-do-boats-float/
Why do boats float? Watch a short video to find out!

World War II: Aircraft Carriers
www.ducksters.com/history/world_war_ii/aircraft_carriers_in_ww2.php
Learn about the aircraft carriers of World War II at this site, including photos and fun facts.

BOOKS

Fox, Tahna Desond. *My Daddy Is a Sailor*. Canon City, CO: Lionheart Group Publishing, 2018.

Loh-Hagen, Virginia. *Aircraft Carriers*. Ann Arbor, MI: Cherry Lake Publishing, 2017.

Publisher's note to parents and teachers: Our editors have reviewed the websites listed here to make sure they're suitable for students. However, websites may change frequently. Please note that students should always be supervised when they access the internet.

INDEX